# CAPTAIN RAPTOR

## and the MOON MYSTERY

### KEVIN O'MALLEY

### Illustrations by PATRICK O'BRIEN

HIGH ABOVE THE PLANET JURASSICA, A *FLASH OF LIGHT* RACES ACROSS THE SKY AND DISAPPEARS ON THE DARK SIDE OF *EON*, THE PLANET'S MOST *MYSTERIOUS* MOON.

THE SCIENTISTS SAY THAT THEY MUST *INVESTIGATE.*

THE GENERALS SAY THAT THEY MUST *PREPARE FOR AN INVASION.*

THE PRESIDENT OF JURASSICA SAYS THEY MUST CALL . . .

THE USD *MEGATOOTH,*
CAPTAIN RAPTOR'S
MASSIVE SPACESHIP, IS
PREPARED FOR TAKEOFF.

"*SADDLE UP,* FOLKS. NO TIME FOR TALKIN'. SOMETHING'S
HAPPENING UP ON EON. *WE'VE GOT A JOB TO DO!*"

CAPTAIN RAPTOR SETS THE ROCKET'S PLASMOCONTROLS FOR *BLASTOFF*. WITH A TREMENDOUS ROAR THE MIGHTY *MEGATOOTH* LIFTS OFF AND *RACES* UP THROUGH THE CLOUDS OF JURASSICA.

"WITHIN THE HOUR WE WILL BE LANDING ON THE SURFACE OF EON. I DON'T WANT ANY SURPRISES, SO *LET'S BE READY* FOR ANYTHING."

NAVIGATOR FIRST CLASS THREETOE PLOTS A COURSE ACROSS THE RUGGED TERRAIN OF EON.

PROFESSOR ANGLEOPTOROUS PREPARES THE PLANETARY SCANNERS.

MASTER SERGEANT BRICKTHOROUS CHECKS HIS NEWEST WEAPON, AN *ULTRANET WEBFLINGER*.

SLOWLY THE *MEGATOOTH* DESCENDS THROUGH THE ELECTRICALLY CHARGED ATMOSPHERE OF THE MOON OF EON. *THUNDER CRASHES* AND JAGGED BOLTS OF *LIGHTNING* CROSS THE SKY.

SUDDENLY . . .

"CAPTAIN, WE'VE BEEN HIT!" CRIES THE PROFESSOR.

"*EVERYONE TO THEIR STATIONS AND BUCKLE UP!*" ORDERS CAPTAIN RAPTOR. "I'M LOSING CONTROL OF THE FORWARD ENGINES. REVERSE ENGINES ARE OFF-LINE. HOLD ON TIGHT FOLKS—*WE'RE GOING IN THE HARD WAY!*"

COULD THIS BE **THE END** OF CAPTAIN RAPTOR AND HIS BRAVE CREW?

THE MIGHTY *MEGATOOTH* **SLAMS** INTO THE RAGING SEA . . . AND IS TOSSED ABOUT LIKE A TOY.

*"WE CAN'T TAKE TOO MUCH MORE OF THIS POUNDING!"* SHOUTS CAPTAIN RAPTOR. "CONVERT THE SHIP TO UNDERSEA MODE. ON MY ORDER . . .

*. . . DIVE, DIVE, DIVE!"*

WITH THE ENGINES DAMAGED, THE *MEGATOOTH* SINKS QUIETLY TOWARD THE BOTTOM OF THE DARK SEAS OF EON.

"PROFESSOR, I NEED YOU TO GET THOSE ENGINES BACK UP AND *RUNNING!*"

"I'M WORKING AS FAST AS I CAN, CAPTAIN. GIVE ME *A FEW MORE MINUTES!*"

"CAPTAIN, I'M DETECTING A *STRANGE* ENERGY SIGNAL FROM AN OBJECT ON THE SEAFLOOR. IT'S LIKE NOTHING I'VE EVER SEEN."

"OKAY THREETOE, WE'LL TAKE A LOOK AT IT WHEN WE GET MOVING."

LITTLE DOES THE FEARLESS CREW SUSPECT THE *HORRIFYING SURPRISE* THAT CREEPS THROUGH THE INKY DEPTHS TOWARD THE SHIP.

# OctoColossus!

THE DREADED BEAST OF THE SEA OF EON SLOWLY WRAPS ITS *GIANT TENTACLES* AROUND THE *MEGATOOTH.*

"CAPTAIN, *THE SHIP CAN'T TAKE THE PRESSURE.* THE MONSTER IS *SQUEEZING US* LIKE A TUBE OF TOOTHPASTE!"

COULD **THIS** BE THE END OF CAPTAIN RAPTOR AND HIS FEARLESS CREW?

"SETTLE DOWN EVERYONE. PROFESSOR, RIG UP AN ELECTROPHOTONIC PULSE AND RUN IT THROUGH THE HULL OF THE SHIP. LET'S GIVE OLD OCTY *A LESSON IN MANNERS.*"

PROFESSOR ANGLEOPTOROUS MAKES THE CONNECTION WITH THE HULL OF THE SHIP AND . . .

ZAP!

THE *SHOCK* IS TOO MUCH FOR THE BEAST. OCTOCOLOSSUS RELEASES ITS GRIP AND SLINKS AWAY.

"NEXT TIME *KEEP YOUR SUCKERS TO YOURSELF.*"

"OKAY CREW, LET'S NOT WAIT AROUND TO SEE IF THE BEAST COMES BACK. THREETOE, WE'RE GOING TO CHECK OUT THAT STRANGE ENERGY SOURCE YOU FOUND DOWN THERE."

THE *MEGATOOTH* RELEASES THE MINISUB AND PROFESSOR ANGLEOPTOROUS MANEUVERS IT SLOWLY TO THE SEAFLOOR.

"FASCINATING," SAYS ANGLEOPTEROUS. "IT APPEARS TO BE SOME SORT OF ENGINE."

GINGERLY HE NUDGES THE OBJECT WITH THE MINISUB'S ROBOT ARMS, THEN PICKS IT UP AND CARRIES IT BACK TO THE *MEGATOOTH*.

OVER THE RIVER OF HYDROPHILLUS AND AROUND THE CLIFFS OF ACROPHOBIUS, THE CREW OF THE *MEGATOOTH* MARCH DEEP INTO THE *UNKNOWN WILDERNESS* OF EON.

FROM THE CREST OF A ROCKY RIDGE, THE CREW SPOT SOMETHING *STRANGE* IN THE VALLEY BELOW. THREETOE RAISES HIS MAGNIVIEWER FOR A CLOSER LOOK.

"*IT'S A SPACESHIP*," HE SAYS, "AND IT LOOKS LIKE IT CRASH-LANDED. *WAIT A MINUTE*—THERE ARE SOME KIND OF *WEIRD CREATURES* DOWN THERE! THEY HAVE NO SCALES, NO HORNS, AND THEY DON'T EVEN HAVE *TAILS!*"

"FASCINATING," SAYS THE PROFESSOR.

CAPTAIN RAPTOR TAKES THE MAGNIVIEWER AND *PEERS SILENTLY* AT THE ALIENS. SUDDENLY HE STANDS UP AND STARTS DOWN THE STEEP SLOPE.

"LET'S FIND OUT WHO, OR WHAT, HAS DROPPED IN. BUT *BE CAREFUL.* I DON'T LIKE THE LOOKS OF THEM, *THEY COULD BE DANGEROUS.*"

CAPTAIN RAPTOR AND HIS CREW PUSH THROUGH THE DARK AND TANGLED JUNGLE, THEN STEP SUDDENLY INTO A CLEARING. THE ALIENS ARE STARTLED. SOME REACH FOR THEIR WEAPONS, WHILE OTHERS STARE IN SHOCK. NO ONE DARES MOVE.

THE JUNGLE HEAT BEGINS TO FEEL LIKE AN INFERNO. SWEAT RUNS DOWN THE ALIENS' SMOOTH SKIN.

NO ONE NOTICES AS A *HUGE, MENACING SHADOW* PASSES OVER THE CLEARING.

SUDDENLY A **GIANT PTERASPIKADON** SWOOPS IN LOW, ITS **MASSIVE CLAWS** HANGING BELOW ITS LONG, SCALY WINGS. IT **GRABS** AN ALIEN AND SOARS INTO THE SKY.

THE ALIENS ON THE GROUND **FIRE WILDLY** AT THE FLEEING MONSTER.

"*HOLD YOUR FIRE!*" SAYS CAPTAIN RAPTOR, AND HE GRABS HIS BLASTOBOOSTER AND *ROCKETS* INTO THE SKY.

RACING UP TO THE BEAST, HE LANDS *A TERRIFIC UPPERCUT* TO ITS JAW.

STUNNED, THE MONSTER LETS OUT A **TERRIFYING ROAR** AND WRAPS ITS WINGS AROUND CAPTAIN RAPTOR AND THE ALIEN. TANGLED TOGETHER, THEY **FALL TOWARD THE SEA**. AN ENORMOUS **SPLASH!** . . . AND THEY'RE GONE.

COULD **THIS** BE THE END OF CAPTAIN RAPTOR?

CAPTAIN RAPTOR LANDS IN THE CLEARING. THE ALIEN SLOWLY CLIMBS OFF HIS BACK. CAUTIOUSLY, CAPTAIN RAPTOR EXTENDS HIS HAND.

"I AM CAPTAIN RAPTOR OF THE PLANET JURASSICA."

THE ALIEN GRASPS THE SCALY HAND. "CAPTAIN STORM, OF THE PLANET EARTH."

"CAPTAIN RAPTOR, WE MEAN YOUR PLANET NO HARM. WE WERE ON A MISSION TO A FAR-OFF GALAXY WHEN OUR SHIP WAS STRUCK BY A METEOR SHOWER. WE HAD TO JETTISON OUR INTERSTELLAR DRIVE."

"I'M AFRAID WE'RE *STUCK* HERE UNTIL WE CAN FIGURE OUT HOW TO BUILD A NEW ONE."

"CAPTAIN STORM, TODAY IS YOUR *LUCKY DAY*. I BELIEVE OUR PROFESSOR HAS WHAT YOU NEED. IS *THIS* BY ANY CHANCE YOUR INTERSTELLAR DRIVE?"

A *CHEER* GOES UP FROM THE ALIEN CREW.

"CAPTAIN RAPTOR, I'M IN YOUR DEBT. YOU SAVED MY SHIP AND MY LIFE. PERHAPS ON OUR RETURN THIS WAY WE COULD MEET AGAIN AND LEARN A BIT MORE ABOUT EACH OTHER."

"IT WOULD BE AN *HONOR*, CAPTAIN STORM."

AS THE DINOSAURS BOARD THE *MEGATOOTH*, CAPTAIN RAPTOR WATCHES THE ALIENS' SPACESHIP FLY OFF AND FINALLY DISAPPEAR ABOVE THE SKIES OF EON.

"PROFESSOR, SEND A REPORT BACK TO JURASSICA. TELL THEM TO TAKE IT EASY. THE SITUATION HERE IS *UNDER CONTROL*."

"BACK TO JURASSICA, CAPTAIN?"
"NO NEED TO HURRY HOME, THREETOE. IT'S A BIG UNIVERSE OUT THERE AND I'M IN THE MOOD FOR ***ADVENTURE***. FIRE UP THE SERVOROCKETS . . ."
***"ONWARD TO THE STARS!"***

TEXT COPYRIGHT © 2005 BY KEVIN O'MALLEY
ILLUSTRATIONS COPYRIGHT © 2005 BY PATRICK O'BRIEN

FIRST PUBLISHED IN THE UNITED STATES OF AMERICA IN 2005 BY
WALKER PUBLISHING COMPANY, INC.

PUBLISHED SIMULTANEOUSLY IN CANADA BY
FITZHENRY AND WHITESIDE, MARKHAM, ONTARIO L3R 4T8

FOR INFORMATION ABOUT PERMISSION TO REPRODUCE SELECTIONS FROM
THIS BOOK, WRITE TO PERMISSIONS, WALKER & COMPANY,
104 FIFTH AVENUE, NEW YORK, NEW YORK 10011

LIBRARY OF CONGRESS CATALOGING-IN-PUBLICATION DATA

O'MALLEY, KEVIN, 1961-
CAPTAIN RAPTOR AND THE MOON MYSTERY / KEVIN O'MALLEY; ILLUSTRATIONS BY PATRICK O'BRIEN.
P. CM.
SUMMARY: WHEN SOMETHING LANDS ON ONE OF THE MOONS OF THE PLANET JURASSICA,
CAPTAIN RAPTOR AND HIS SPACESHIP CREW GO TO INVESTIGATE.
ISBN 0-8027-8935-8 — ISBN 0-8027-8936-6
[1. DINOSAURS-FICTION. 2. HEROES-FICTION. 3. MYSTERY AND DETECTIVE STORIES.
4. SCIENCE FICTION.] I. O'BRIEN, PATRICK, 1960- ILL. II. TITLE.

PZ7.0526CA 2005
[E]—DC22
2004053624

THE ARTIST USED WATERCOLOR AND GOUACHE ON PAPER
TO CREATE THE ILLUSTRATIONS FOR THIS BOOK.

BOOK DESIGN BY PATRICK O'BRIEN

VISIT WALKER & COMPANY'S WEB SITE AT WWW.WALKERYOUNGREADERS.COM

PRINTED IN HONG KONG

2 4 6 8 10 9 7 5 3 1